Dee and Me

Written by Lois Bick
Illustrated by Sally Springer

My sister Dee wants to do all the things that I can do.

I can make my bed.

Dee likes to make her bed, too.

She says she can do it all by herself.

But sometimes she needs a little help.

I can sweep the floor.

Dee likes to sweep the floor, too.

She says she can do it all by herself.

But sometimes she needs a little help.

I can dress myself.

Dee likes to dress herself, too.

She says she can do it all by herself.

But sometimes she needs a little help.

I can brush my teeth.

Dee likes to brush her teeth, too.

She says she can do it all by herself.

But sometimes she needs a little help.

What a mess!

I can feed our pet mouse.

Dee likes to feed our pet, too.

She says she can do it all by herself.

But sometimes she needs a little help.

14

I can eat all my dinner.

Then I can have pie.

Dee likes pie, too.

She says she can eat it all by herself.

And do you know what?

She NEVER needs any help!